THE BOOK THAT JACK WROTE

Written by Jon Scieszka
Paintings by Daniel Adel

VIKING

This is the Book that Jack wrote.

THE BOOK
THAT
JACK WROTE

Written by Jon Scieszka
Paintings by Daniel Adel

This is the Picture

That lay in the Book that Jack wrote.

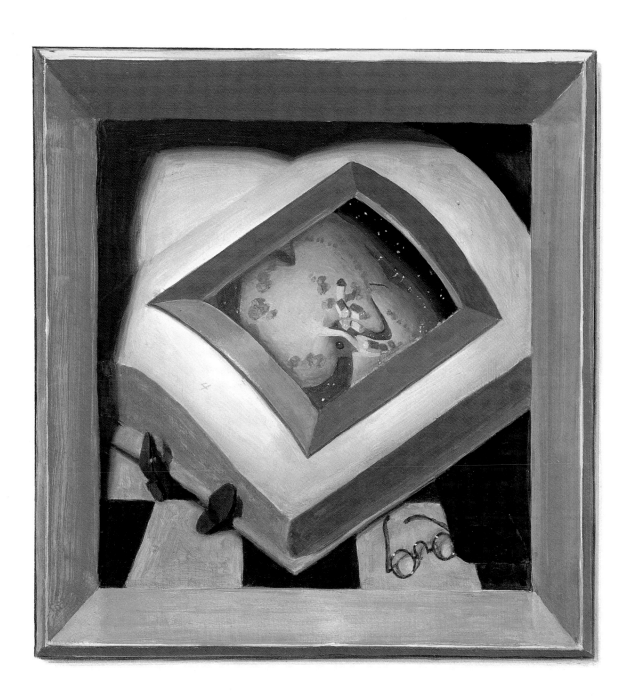

This is the Rat,

That fell in the Picture

That lay in the Book that Jack wrote.

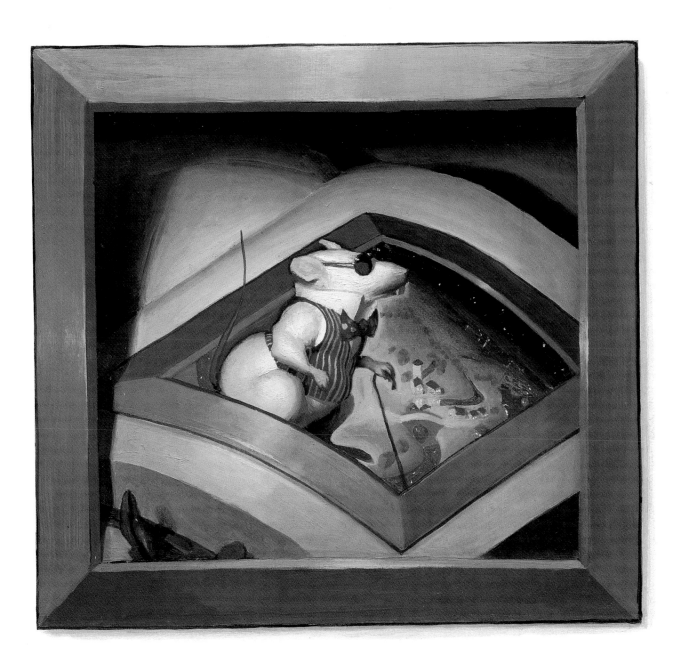

This is the Cat,
That ate the Rat,
That fell in the Picture
That lay in the Book that Jack wrote.

This is the Dog,

That chased the Cat,

That ate the Rat,

That fell in the Picture

That lay in the Book that Jack wrote.

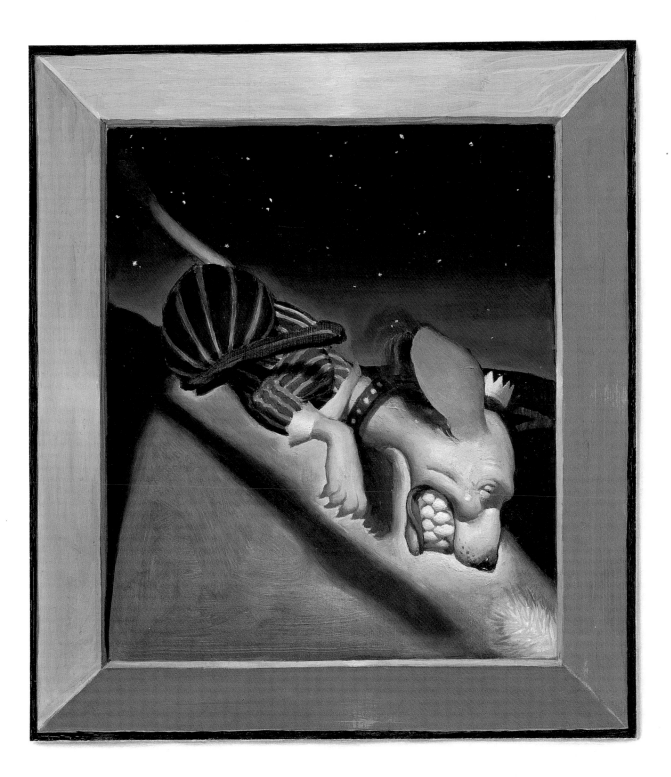

This is the Cow sailing over the moon,

That spooked the Dog,

That chased the Cat,

That ate the Rat,

That fell in the Picture

That lay in the Book that Jack wrote.

This is the Baby humming the tune,

That tossed the Cow sailing over the moon,

That spooked the Dog,

That chased the Cat,

That ate the Rat,

That fell in the Picture

That lay in the Book that Jack wrote.

This is the Pie flying through the air,

That beaned the Baby humming the tune,

That tossed the Cow sailing over the moon,

That spooked the Dog,

That chased the Cat,

That ate the Rat,

That fell in the Picture

That lay in the Book that Jack wrote.

This is the Pieman at the fair,

That flung the Pie flying through the air,

That beaned the Baby humming the tune,

That tossed the Cow sailing over the moon,

That spooked the Dog,

That chased the Cat,

That ate the Rat,

That fell in the Picture

That lay in the Book that Jack wrote.

This is the Egg falling off the wall,

That startled the Pieman at the fair,

That flung the Pie flying through the air,

That beaned the Baby humming the tune,

That tossed the Cow sailing over the moon,

That spooked the Dog,

That chased the Cat,

That ate the Rat,

That fell in the Picture

That lay in the Book that Jack wrote.

PIES

This is the Hatter in the hall,

That knocked the Egg falling off the wall,

That startled the Pieman at the fair,

That flung the Pie flying through the air,

That beaned the Baby humming the tune,

That tossed the Cow sailing over the moon,

That spooked the Dog,

That chased the Cat,

That ate the Rat,

That fell in the Picture

That lay in the Book that Jack wrote.

This is the Bug, that frayed the rug,

That tripped the Hatter in the hall,

That knocked the Egg falling off the wall,

That startled the Pieman at the fair,

That flung the Pie flying through the air,

That beaned the Baby humming the tune,

That tossed the Cow sailing over the moon,

That spooked the Dog,

That chased the Cat,

That ate the Rat,

That fell in the Picture

That lay in the Book that Jack wrote.

This is the Man in the tattered coat,

That stomped the Bug, that frayed the rug,

That tripped the Hatter in the hall,

That knocked the Egg falling off the wall,

That startled the Pieman at the fair,

That flung the Pie flying through the air,

That beaned the Baby humming the tune,

That tossed the Cow sailing over the moon,

That spooked the Dog,

That chased the Cat,

That ate the Rat,

That fell in the Picture

That lay in the Book that Jack wrote.

This is the Book that Jack wrote,

That squashed the Man in the tattered coat,

That stomped the Bug, that frayed the rug,

That tripped the Hatter in the hall,

That knocked the Egg falling off the wall,

That startled the Pieman at the fair,

That flung the Pie flying through the air,

That beaned the Baby humming the tune,

That tossed the Cow sailing over the moon,

That spooked the Dog,

That chased the Cat,

That ate the Rat,

That fell in the Picture ...

Written by Jon Scieszka
Paintings by Daniel Adel

That lay in the Book that Jack wrote.

To Regina Hayes
J.S.

To Ninotchka and the Parkenheimer
D.Q.A.

VIKING
Published by the Penguin Group
Penguin Books USA Inc., 375 Hudson Street, New York, New York 10014, U.S.A.
Penguin Books Ltd, 27 Wrights Lane, London W8 5TZ, England
Penguin Books Australia Ltd, Ringwood, Victoria, Australia
Penguin Books Canada Ltd, 10 Alcorn Avenue, Toronto, Ontario, Canada M4V 3B2
Penguin Books (N.Z.) Ltd, 182-190 Wairau Road, Auckland 10, New Zealand

Penguin Books Ltd, Registered Offices: Harmondsworth, Middlesex, England

First published by Viking, a division of Penguin Books USA Inc., 1994

3 5 7 9 10 8 6 4 2

Text copyright © Jon Scieszka, 1994
Illustrations copyright © Daniel Adel, 1994
All rights reserved

LIBRARY OF CONGRESS CATALOGING-IN-PUBLICATION DATA
Scieszka, Jon.
The book that Jack wrote/Jon Scieszka;
illustrated by Daniel Adel.   p.   cm.
Summary: a madcap variation of the cumulative
nursery rhyme, this time beginning when Jack writes a book.
ISBN 0-670-84330-X
1. Nursery rhymes.   2. Children's poetry.   [1. Nursery rhymes.]
I. Adel, Daniel, ill. II. House that Jack built.   III. Title.
PZ8.3.S347Bo 1994
811'.54—dc20   94-10932   CIP   AC

Printed in the U.S.A.

Set in Bernhart

Printed on recycled paper.

Book Design: Jeri Hansen, New York, New York
Marbled Design © Mimi Schleicher, 1994
Weaverville, North Carolina

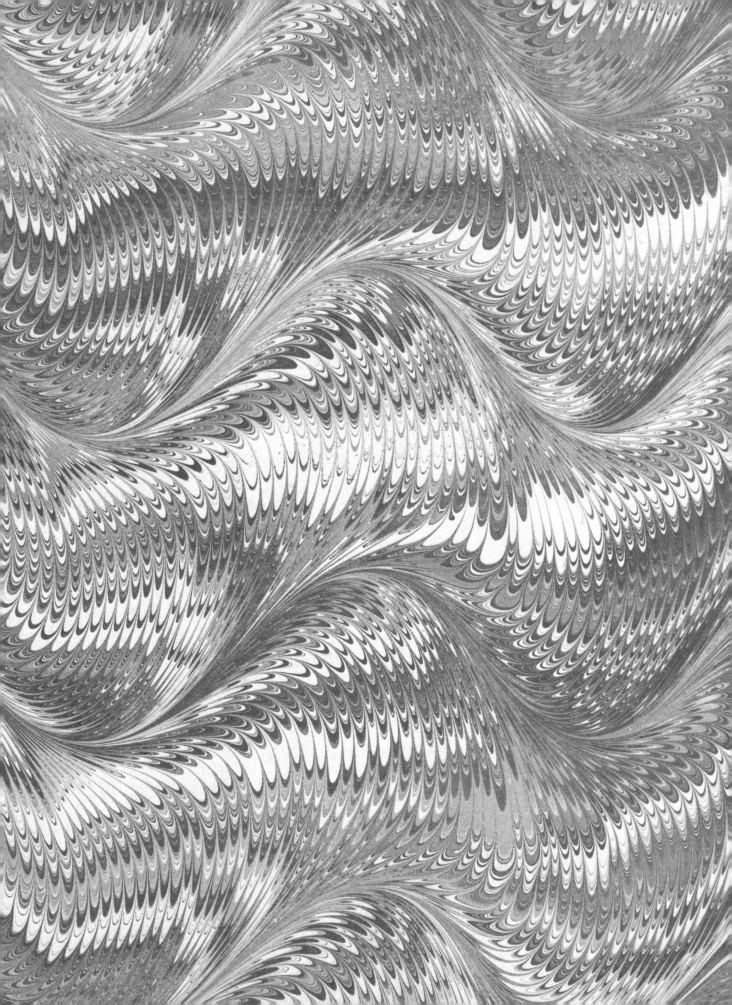